DARCY INTERRUPTED

A PRIDE AND PREJUDICE SENSUAL VARIATION

DEMI MONDE

DEDICATION

I would like to thank Debra-Ann Kummoung for the butler's name, Rebecca Payne and Beatrice Nearey for the valet's name, and Gail Frisby for the maid's name.

They are members of my Facebook group Pride and Prejudice Variations.

CHAPTER 1

ELIZABETH GRABBED Mr. Darcy's hand as they rounded the corner of the long drive and Pemberley finally came into view. She inhaled and squeezed his hand so hard that it must have hurt. The building and the estate were still stunning, just as magnificent as the first time she had seen it with her aunt and uncle that fateful day.

"Do you still approve?"

She heard a note of humor in his question. It was nearly the same question he had asked the last and only other time she had been at Pemberley. Elizabeth dragged her eyes away from the view and focused on her husband.

"Yes." Words were not enough to convey all she felt at seeing that grand estate, sitting next to the man she loved, the man who owned that house and had driven her to distraction these last three days of travel.

Mr. Darcy's lips turned up at the corners, and his gaze changed from happiness to a deeper and more primal emotion. Elizabeth licked her lips at the desire she saw in his eyes. They had teased each other mercilessly on this trip. He had to teach her how to tease, which she had learned at a rapid pace. Both had wanted to wait until they reached Pemberley to consummate their marriage.

And now that they were here...

Mr. Darcy pulled her hand towards him, holding her on his lap as she fell on him. Elizabeth did not even wait to situate herself before she reached for his curly hair, squeezed a handful and put her mouth on his. One of his large hands was on her back, the other squeezing her rump. His hot mouth, inquisitive tongue, and groans drove her wild.

During the trip to Derbyshire, she had learned all sorts of new things about her husband, most of all what drove him wild. She learned about herself as well and what she enjoyed, though he promised her there was more, much more to learn. They had had to redirect their attention from consummating the marriage in the carriage and so to distract themselves, they had talked of what they knew and loved.

Elizabeth blushed at the noise she had just made. She could not help it: his hand was on her left breast, kneading it. She moved her rump to have a better angle to kiss and run her hands down his face. Mr. Darcy's long groan nearly had her stop, but he had taught her in the last few days that it was not a groan of pain, but of exquisite pleasure.

"Oh my love, you will have me unfit to meet the staff."

The breathy statement against her neck penetrated her fevered mind, and she stopped her kisses, then sat up.

Mr. Darcy stared at her heavy lidded, eyes glazed, mouth agape and breathing heavily. Her bosom rapidly rose and fell with her breaths, drawing her husband's gaze. She blushed again with the widest smile. The quite proper Mr. Darcy had come completely undone with her kiss. This must be what a hunter feels like bagging the biggest bird, she thought.

"You seem quite proud of yourself, Mrs. Darcy."

She chuckled and put her hands on his shoulders again. "I am. The great, proud, proper Mr. Darcy has come undone by a simple kiss."

He rose his eyebrows and scoffed. "That was no simple kiss. You were touching me and making the most divine noises of pleasure."

Elizabeth raised her hands, intending to cover her face, but he caught them in his grasp and did not let go. "You have nothing to be embarrassed about. I am very happy to hear those noises. To have you squirming in my lap, driven wild by my kisses."

Elizabeth arched an eyebrow. "*Your* kisses? Why sir, I believe you stated it was *my* kisses that drove you undone?"

Mr. Darcy chuckled and then froze as the carriage stopped. Elizabeth raised her head in horror. They were at the front steps of Pemberley, and she was astride Mr. Darcy like a wanton lightskirt.

He picked her up and set her next to him, and they both proceeded to straighten their clothes, run hands over their hair, and do whatever they could to make themselves presentable. It would not do for the new mistress of Pemberley to meet the staff looking like she had been nearly ravished in the carriage. Even if she had.

MR. DARCY COULD NOT KEEP THE SMALL SMILE OFF his countenance as he adjusted his vest, coat, and cravat. Elizabeth, his wife, was no cold fish. She melted at his touch, could not get enough of his kisses. He grinned and wished he could show off his wife to everyone and crow that he had found the best woman, intelligent, kind, and best of all, she craved his touch.

He glanced at Elizabeth, who was patting her hair back into place. It was obvious that they were not perfectly presentable, but perhaps the servants would attribute that to being in the carriage all day. If not, well... he did not mind if they thought Mr. and Mrs. Darcy had a happy marriage.

His grin grew even bigger, and he opened the door to the carriage. The footman was still there, having knocked several minutes before. The lad was a good servant, though, and kept his face blank.

Mr. Darcy turned back, offering his hand to Elizabeth. She held onto his hand as she stepped down from the carriage and saw the grand estate not as a day visitor but as the mistress. She inhaled and looked up, then left to right as her eyes widened. The number of servants at Pemberley was prodigious. An estate this size needed many servants, and all were lined up in two rows from the carriage to the steps.

He tucked Elizabeth's arm in his and nodded to Mrs. Reynolds the housekeeper, who then stepped forward and curtsied. "Greetings, Mrs. Darcy. I am Mrs. Reynolds, the housekeeper. I am quite happy you are finally here."

He felt so proud of his wife and of the wonderful greeting that he almost burst. From despairing to ever find a woman, to finding and losing her, to winning her back and marrying her—his emotions were threatening to overcome him. He would need a stiff drink, or he would probably cry from joy.

Mr. Darcy escorted Elizabeth down the lines of servants. She said something nice and smiled at every servant, and there were a large number. By the end of the second line he could tell she was tiring, as her smile was forced and she was fidgeting often.

"Mrs. Reynolds, could you have a bath drawn for my wife and myself and brought to our rooms? I am sure Mrs. Darcy would like to rest and wash off the day's travel."

Elizabeth turned towards him with love in her eyes and a smile. He grinned again at her, unable to stop smiling. He could not imagine ever not smiling now that he had his love at his home. She squeezed his arm, then they both walked up the steps to enter Pemberley, but he stopped Elizabeth and turned back, ignoring her quizzical gaze.

"Mr. Jameson, could you hold open the door? I shall be unable to do so."

He turned back to his love with a grin and then smirked at her furrowed brow and open mouth, probably to ask why he would be unable to open a door. He bent his knees and swooped her in his arms and stood ready to cross the threshold with his bride.

Elizabeth laughed with her arms around his neck. He beamed so wide his cheeks hurt and stepped across the threshold of Pemberley as the servants cheered and whooped. He was finally home with Elizabeth.

CHAPTER 2

MR. DARCY SNEAKED a quick peck on her lips before the servants walked further into the house. She hid her countenance on his chest as the staff filed past to return to their duties.

"The baths will be ready right away. Shall I send up a tray with a light meal?"

She felt the rumble of his voice as he answered Mrs. Reynolds. Elizabeth was too embarrassed to straighten up and face the housekeeper after she had been hiding in Mr. Darcy's chest. Plus, it was so nice to be standing so close to him that she did not want to move. His arms were wrapped around her back, and she held onto his coat.

"Should I carry you up the steps to your bedchamber, Mrs. Darcy?" His hot breath tickled her scalp.

She shook her head.

"Are all the servants gone?" She was such a ninny.

She could feel his chuckle through his chest. That may be her new favorite place to rest her head.

"Yes, except for Mrs. Reynolds and the Mr. Jameson. Should I have them look away?"

She peeked an eye out and saw that both servants were busy looking elsewhere, so she raised her eyes and delivered a flat stare at her husband. Which was ruined by the upturn of her lips. She turned away, Mr. Darcy caught her hand, and they both walked up the staircase holding hands.

They parted at their separate bedchambers, but not before sharing longing looks that set her cheeks on fire. She entered her new bedchamber with a smile and desire in her eyes.

"Oh!" The room was beautifully done in pastels of rose and yellow, happy colors that Elizabeth loved. How did he know? He could not have ordered her bedchamber redone before they had arrived, could he? She would have to ask. He had been so pleasing during their courtship and engagement that she would not put it past him.

A large four poster bed took up the majority of the room, but there was still enough space left for a screen with a tub in a corner, a sitting area with a sofa and chairs, a writing desk, and a vanity, as well as a wardrobe. Elizabeth turned to take it all in with a hand upon her chest. She would have been happy with any colors and furniture, truth be told, but this was almost right out of one of her girlish dreams. The only missing piece was a bookshelf full of books.

A knock at the door interrupted her musings. "Come in."

A maid entered and curtsied. "Pardon, Mistress, but the hot water is here for your bath."

Elizabeth nodded, and the maid opened the door to let in several servants with pitchers of steaming water. Her hot bath was ready in less than a minute. Never had she had such fast service. No wonder Mr. Darcy had looked down at everything in the country if this was what real living among the upper class was like.

Her maid, Agatha, helped her undress, but Elizabeth declined the offer of help to wash. That was one thing she could do herself and would not give up. She could employ Agatha to pour water over her hair, though. Her maid stayed on the other side of the screen while Elizabeth washed herself with the divine rose scented soap. She leaned back, relaxed against the tub, and sighed.

The hot water felt so good on her tired and sore muscles. The roads were full of holes and ruts, and even though Mr. Darcy's carriages were well sprung, travel was still a tedious and painful business. Elizabeth sighed again and slipped down farther into the steaming bath, closing her eyes. She would have pinched herself to determine this was not a dream but was too content to move.

She thought back to their engagement and the weeks before they married. Elizabeth smiled at the memories. Mr. Darcy was not the staid and formal man the world knew him as. Imagine if everyone was privy to this man, especially Miss Bingley, of how amorous he was, how clever he was at finding seconds to steal kisses.

Her favorite memory was when Mr. Darcy had walked into the garden and offered to help pick and hang the flowers and herbs. Elizabeth giggled at how naïve she had been. He had leaned down next to her, trailing his fingers up her leg, almost reaching her hip before he put his hand down. Or how he had handed his herbs to her chest, so when she had taken them, he had run a finger along the edge of her breast. Or how when she had held up the lavender stems and tied them to the ceiling hook, Mr. Darcy had steadied her with his hands sliding along her waist and down her hips.

He had driven her to distraction in public, with her sister in attendance. Never had his countenance given away what he had been doing, except for a sly wink that no one else had seen.

She could not wait for that evening to consummate their marriage.

MR. DARCY WALKED INTO HIS BEDCHAMBER WITH A smile. Finally, he was home, and with Elizabeth as his wife, as he had dreamed.

He pulled at his cravat and then stood still to let his valet, Mr. Simkin, undress him. That was for the best, as his mind was most certainly not on his clothes or even anything in this room. His lips curled up as he thought of his new bride undressing and taking her bath. He heard Mr. Simkin cough and realized he had better stop thinking of Elizabeth while his valet was assisting in removing his clothes.

With his robe on, Mr. Simkin opened the door to the servants carrying buckets of steaming water. This was near the top of a list of what he missed about Pemberley while he had been in Hertfordshire. He stepped into his over large tub and sank down. No bath at Netherfield or any inn was as big as his at Pemberley.

Mr. Darcy rested his head on the edge of the bathing tub and closed his eyes, letting the hot water sooth his aching muscles. There was one muscle in particular that was sore. He had vowed to not relieve himself after they were married, but he was not sure he had completely thought that through. He was randy, and Elizabeth was untouched, and from their conversations and teasing the last several weeks, he knew she did not know much if anything regarding the marriage bed. Would he not take care with her if he was too aroused from being denied release for so long?

He picked up the bar of soap and lathered his chest and arms. Then he scrubbed most of the rest of his body. He rubbed the bar between his hands to build up a good lather, then washed between his legs. That was a bad decision, as he had already had a cockstand, and with his hand sliding up and down his shaft he groaned.

Would it not be kinder to relieve the pressure, so to speak, so he could take care and make Elizabeth's first time not be painful?

Each squeezing stroke pulled deeper groans. He imagined his wife in her tub, scrubbing her skin with the soap he had picked out especially for her. Her lathered hands rubbing her breasts. He lifted his hips, stroking—

His bedchamber door burst open. "Sir, your aunt, Lady Catherine de Bourgh, is in the sitting room."

All the air rushed out of his lungs as he fell back in the tub. His cockstand shriveled as he held it, still in shock over his valet's statement.

"My aunt," Mr. Darcy coughed, "My aunt is here? Downstairs?"

"Yes. Mr. Jameson did his best to direct her elsewhere, but she brushed him aside and entered. She stated that she will not leave until she sees you. What would you have me do, sir?"

Mr. Darcy growled and ducked his head as he poured bathwater over it. Of all the times, of all the days for her to make an unexpected visit to Pemberley. He raised his eyes. "Does my aunt know that my wife, my new bride, and I just arrived here ourselves?"

"Yes, sir."

"And does she also know that we were married a few days past?"

"She does, sir. She did mention it."

Mr. Darcy narrowed his eyes. Then he clenched his teeth and stood up. "Tell her that I am currently indisposed and unable to receive her. She will have to stay at the closest inn, which I believe is in Lambton."

He stepped out of the tub, grabbing his towel off of the screen. He would have to dress quickly, as he knew his aunt would not listen to his order. She would probably storm the house looking for him. He clenched his teeth as his valet gave his orders to a footman and returned to help Mr. Darcy dress. Lady Catherine de Bourgh had gone too far this time.

His hair still damp, Mr. Darcy walked to his bedchamber entrance to face his mother's sister. His valet opened the door to show Mr. Jameson in the process of knocking.

"Where is he? Where is my nephew?" His aunt's commanding voice could be heard even down the hall on the second floor.

Mr. Darcy turned his narrowed eyes on his butler.

"She has been demanding to speak with you, sir. She refuses to stay at an inn."

Mr. Darcy nodded, his mouth flat and pinched. He stepped past Mr. Jameson to walk down the hallway towards the main staircase and his aunt.

CHAPTER 3

ELIZABETH'S pleasant thoughts were disturbed by the knocking on her husband's bedroom door. She closed her eyes again and settled back to soak, sure that the servants had questions since he had just arrived home at Pemberley after a few months. But they sprang open again at the muffled shouting that seemed to come from far away in the house.

She sat up and called for her maid. "Do you know what the disturbance is?"

"No, mistress, I do not. Would you like me to find out?"

Elizabeth opened her mouth, paused, and then spoke. "Is Mr. Darcy usually interrupted this much after he returns home?"

"Not that I can recall. He is generally left alone until the next day. He wants to rest before he deals with the estate."

Elizabeth frowned and bit the inside of her cheek. She had not expected anything to interfere with their first night at her new home and indeed had hoped it would not. She did not know what was happening, but she was not going to be found in her bath if there was an emergency.

She stood and asked for the towels from her maid. Agatha offered to dry her, but Elizabeth declined. The tasks the servants at Pemberley did were definitely more than Hill ever did at Longbourn, she noted.

Agatha held out Elizabeth's bedclothes.

Elizabeth shook her head. "I want to find out what is happening. Bring me my blue dress."

The muffled yelling again caught her attention. This time it sounded closer. Elizabeth and the maid exchanged looks. "Agatha, could you go find out what is taking place?"

The maid quickly slipped out the bedchamber while Elizabeth pulled on her chemise. By the time she had her dress on, the girl was back.

"Lady Catherine de Bourgh is here and halfway up the staircase. Mr. Darcy has stopped her from coming any further."

Lady Catherine de Bourgh was here? The woman had not attended their wedding and had not even acknowledged it, except for a letter sent to Mr. Darcy that he had burned immediately before he went out for a long ride by himself. He never had told her its contents, but from what his aunt had said during her unexpected visit to Longbourn, she could imagine quite well what was in the message.

"Quickly, button me up." She had to be with her husband now. Plus, her appearance might cause Lady Catherine to have an apoplexy and induce her to leave immediately.

"If only that would happen."

Agatha looked at Elizabeth with furrowed brows. "Pardon me, mistress?"

"Oh, never mind me. I have a tendency to talk to myself, as you have now found out."

Thankfully Elizabeth's hair had not yet been undone, so she was quickly ready to face down the formidable Lady Catherine de Bourgh.

"If you would follow along in case we need to call for more servants or ride for help."

Elizabeth walked out the door, clearly hearing the disruption now. She imagined anyone within Pemberley could hear it.

"—reprehensible and against all the grand estate, history and power the Darcy name stands for!" A loud bang echoed throughout the entry.

"I am asking you again, Aunt, before I have you thrown out, to please leave immediately."

"I will not go. She has twisted you against your relatives already, just as I had feared! My nephew would never throw his own aunt, only sister of his beloved mother, out of his house—"

"He will if she shows up unannounced and unexpectedly the very evening that he arrives home with his new bride from their several days of travel after their wedding. A wedding that you did not attend."

Elizabeth was now near the top of the staircase and could see Lady Catherine's countenance, which was a deep vermillion and distorted with rage.

Mr. Darcy turned his head to the servant at the bottom of the steps. "Mr. Jameson, can you, along with several footmen, escort my aunt to her carriage? Make sure she leaves at once."

Mr. Jameson climbed the steps and grabbed Lady Catherine's arm before she could even lodge a protest. Other servants darted out from under the balcony to run up the stairs as well. They must have been hiding near the entry and listening. It was embarrassing on her first night at her new home.

"This is preposterous! Horrible!" Lady Catherine tried to dislodge her arms from the servant's hold. "This is no way to treat a relation that has shown nothing but kindness to you. How dare you—"

Mr. Darcy's voice boomed. "You are not welcome here until you apologize to me and to my wife for what you have said and done here tonight!"

Lady Catherine continued to struggle, but the men held on tightly and easily carried her out the doors of Pemberley.

Mr. Darcy let out his breath and ran a hand through his hair. He looked down at the staircase and groaned. Never would he have thought his aunt could behave in such a deplorable manner. He raised his head again and sighed. He felt guilty for treating her so, but what else could he have done?

He turned and wearily climbed the rest of the staircase. He neared the landing, looked up and stopped when he saw Elizabeth standing at the top of the stairs. His shoulders drooped. "I am sorry Elizabeth, for what you heard. I—"

She stepped down until she was on one higher step and placed her hands on his arms. "Fitzwilliam, you are not responsible for your aunt. Do not forget that I have already experienced this side of her when she visited me at Longbourn."

Mr. Darcy searched her countenance. He had forgotten about his aunt's visit to Longbourn, the visit that raised his hopes, that urged him to return to Hertfordshire and call upon Elizabeth again. That gave him hope that perhaps she did not despise him any longer.

"Come, let us enjoy the rest of our evening."

Mr. Darcy slowly smiled as he walked up the steps arm in arm with Elizabeth and down the hallway. He was still embarrassed by his aunt's spectacle but knew his bride would not hold him to blame.

"I hope you did not end your bath early."

Elizabeth looked up at him. "I had a very pleasant soaking. The large tub was wonderful. I could have fallen asleep."

He turned and kissed her cheek, the scent of roses from the soap on her skin smelled divine. "I chose the soap for you. I wanted it to match the new decoration of your room."

"I cannot believe that you were able to get it redecorated so quickly after our engagement."

Mr. Darcy glanced at her while swallowing and running a hand through his hair. It would not have been enough time for the bedchamber to be completely redone. But would she be insulted or think it romantic that he had started the redecoration after his aunt's visit to him? He had such hope, a longing hope that she might be at Pemberley after all, that he had ordered the work done.

"Do you like your bedchamber?"

Elizabeth brought her other hand to rest on his arm. "I love it. It is absolutely charming, and the colors are ones I prefer. I have everything I need, except for perhaps a few books."

Mr. Darcy beamed at the knowledge that he had gotten her room exactly right. "I left the selection of books for you to undertake. There are many in the Pemberley library that you could relocate. Or you can purchase all the volumes you want and make your own library."

Elizabeth squeezed his arm and grinned at him.

In that moment with Elizabeth's beaming gaze upon him, he felt he was the most amazing man in the world. All thoughts of his aunt and her disruption had been completely forgotten. He began to feel those feelings for his wife, the ones that had disappeared so utterly when he heard Lady Catherine had appeared.

Mr. Darcy glanced over at Elizabeth, who was looking down the hall, and lowered his gaze to her long elegant neck... which led to her beautiful bosom. There was not nearly enough of it on display, but he would only allow that in the privacy of their rooms. His pants were uncomfortably tight, so he dragged his eyes away and noticed they were almost to his bedchamber door.

He turned to Elizabeth. "Are you tired and sore and wish to retire and sleep?"

He did not want her first time to be a disaster because of soreness or exhaustion from traveling. No matter how much he longed for her, he would not put his needs above hers. Mr. Darcy was gratified to see a twinkle in his wife's eyes.

She raised her hand and placed it on his chest, causing his heart to beat faster. He fixed his right hand over hers and hoped.

"I do believe, Mr. Darcy, that my hot bath has eased my sore muscles."

CHAPTER 4

ELIZABETH QUICKLY SLIPPED into her bedchamber with a smile and a giggle. She caught her maid turning down her bed and laying her wedding night-dress on it.

"May I help you change?"

Elizabeth nodded and looked away as a blush heated her neck and cheeks. If only she did not need a maid to help her undress and button her clothes. Then no one would know what she and her husband would be doing soon. She bit her bottom lip as she realized that everyone probably knew, as it was their first night in their home after their wedding. She chewed the inside of her cheek and clenched the sides of her dress.

Agatha unbuttoned her and pulled the dress up off

her arms, then her chemise. Her wedding nightdress was exquisite, made from the finest silk. She put on the dress and smoothed her hands over her stomach feeling the smooth fabric. Her maid handed Elizabeth the robe that was also new and matched the nightdress. They were both a pale pink and her only extravagant expenditure for her trousseau. The other dresses and hats she purchased were modest, which was her style.

Elizabeth sat in front of the vanity while Agatha took down her hair and brushed it. Having someone else brush was one of the few pleasures she craved. Plus, her long and curly hair was prone to tangles. Her arms used to get tired brushing and working out the snags every day.

She opened her eyes when the brushing stopped. "Will there be anything else? Do you want me to blow out the candles?"

Elizabeth shook her head. "No, that will be all. Thank you."

She chewed inside of her cheek as she looked around her bedchamber. She did not know whether she should keep the candles lit or blow them out. Elizabeth did not want Fitzwilliam to trip or not be able to find her when he came through the connecting door. But she also preferred the candles not all be lit when he saw her in her nightclothes. She finally decided to blow them out except for the one on the vanity.

Elizabeth climbed into bed and then stopped. Should she lie down or sit up against the headboard? She groaned and looked heavenward. If only she had any notion of what to expect. Fitzwilliam would probably tell her when he came in.

She took her robe off and placed it on the chair next to the bed. Then she scooted down and pulled the covers up to her chin. He would be surprised to find only her head peeking out of the blankets. But having a man see her in this clinging nightdress, even if he was her husband, was embarrassing.

She wished Jane had married earlier so that she could tell Elizabeth what to expect. If only there were some way that she could talk to her sister immediately— but even an express rider would take days. Her mother told them that there would be a pain, but if she lay still it would all be over quickly. She knew Fitzwilliam would not purposely hurt her, but remembering her mother's advice had not calmed her nerves.

The connecting door opened. Elizabeth glanced at it, then immediately looked straight ahead. She was embarrassed to find that she had brought the covers up to her nose.

"Elizabeth?" Mr. Darcy stood just inside her room.

She stared at him, then slowly pushed the blankets below her mouth. "I... I do not know what to expect, so..."

She could feel her cheeks heat again. Elizabeth pulled the blankets up under her nose and closed her eyes. She was utterly embarrassed.

At the sound of chuckling, she opened them and glared at her husband approaching her bed. He had a robe covering his nightshirt. She noticed chest hair out peeking out, quickly swallowed and looked away to stare across the room. Her heart was beating so rapidly it was liable to jump out of her chest.

"Are you frightened?"

Elizabeth kept staring straight ahead while biting the inside of her cheek. Should she tell him she did not know what to expect and was scared?

"Do not worry. You already know almost everything that will happen tonight." The bed dipped as he sat on the edge. "As a matter of fact, you have found it quite enjoyable."

Elizabeth turned to Mr. Darcy with a furrowed brow, sure he was addled. She pulled the covers down to under her mouth. "I do?"

Mr. Darcy's lips curved upward as he nodded. "Those kisses we have shared? The touching we have enjoyed?"

He stood, shrugged off his robe and placed it on the chair. Elizabeth quickly gazed at him and stopped where his nightshirt tented out. It was almost on the same level as her eyes. Her blushing renewed with vigor, she turned her head away to stare at the underside of her canopy bed.

MR. DARCY BIT HIS BOTTOM LIP TO STOP ANY laughter bubbling out. He had never had any doubts, but this confirmed that she had absolutely no knowledge of the marriage bed. He was pleased, as he wanted to be the only man who would ever see her disrobed or bring her to pleasure.

Mr. Darcy pulled back the covers. Actually, he tried to pull them down, but Elizabeth held onto them tightly. "Could you move over so that I can get in?"

Elizabeth scooted quickly to the far side of the bed and again drew the blankets up to her eyes. She stared at him as he laid down and pulled the covers up to his chest. Her eyes were almost bulging out of her head. This would not do.

Whatever she had been told by Mrs. Bennet had to have been horrible. It was probably done to keep young women from anticipating their wedding vows. However it had also created the need for him to calm Elizabeth before they could get anywhere near consummating the marriage.

He rolled over on his side and placed a hand on top of the sheets, near her. "Do you remember our kisses?"

Elizabeth nodded, the blankets still pulled up to her eyes.

"Do you recall my touches, when I trailed my fingers along your side?"

He moved those same fingers along her side over the covers, up her arms and shoulders to her chin. He trailed his fingers over her hands holding the covers, around her eyes and through her hair. He did the same action again until Elizabeth lowered the covers. He dragged his fingers around her lips, over her cheek, around her eyes, over her eyebrows and through her hair.

She sighed.

"Did you enjoy that?"

Elizabeth hummed and turned her face towards him.

Mr. Darcy ran his fingertips over her lips, down her cheek, over her jawline around her ear, then down her neck. She lowered the covers to give him more skin to touch. He obliged by trailing his fingers down her long neck to her collarbone, over her shoulders and up her chest. But he still could not access Elizabeth's bosom that had taunted him and featured in many of his dreams since first meeting her.

He moved his fingertips over her upper chest and collarbone. "Would you lower the covers?"

Elizabeth slowly lowered the sheets while staring at him. It was torture watching the blankets gradually expose her bosom, still covered by the nightdress. Finally the bedcovers were down at her waist.

Mr. Darcy drew his fingers again over the sensitive areas on her face. He would gently ease her into having her breasts touched. He did not want to move too fast and have Elizabeth hiding under the covers again.

He swept his finger lightly over her collarbone, down her chest, over her nightdress, on her breast, circling her nipple and then over the other. Elizabeth released a breath as he ran his fingers back up the other side of her neck and began the slow maddening touches again.

It was good that he had left the bedcovers over his waist and lain angled on the bed, as he had a prominent cockstand. He was so ready for her that he hurt. Of course his being interrupted in the bath before had been painful, but he had been able to ignore the pain by focusing on his anger at his aunt.

Slowly his fingers trailed her skin over her nightdress, circling ever closer to her nipple. Finally, he rubbed a nipple, drawing a gasp from Elizabeth. He glanced up and saw she was breathing heavily. His grin grew. He focused on lightly touching her other nipple through the silk. He leaned over and kissed it.

Elizabeth moaned.

Mr. Darcy kissed and dragged his finger around her nipple and breast before moving to pay his respects to her other fine breast. But he did not leave the other one alone. His thumb rubbed her other nipple, causing her to fidget.

"Oh, Fitzwilliam. That feels so divine."

Mr. Darcy looked up at her with heavy-lidded eyes. "This is what will happen tonight. I will make you feel good."

He slipped a few fingers under the strap of her nightdress and slowly pulled it down one shoulder. He did the same to the other but continued to pull it down until her gorgeous breasts were exposed to him. He groaned.

He looked up at Elizabeth, who clutched the covers by her side. "They are beautiful."

The ability to think and speak coherently was quickly leaving him. Still laying on his side, he leaned over her touching, squeezing, kissing both breasts. He lightly ran his fingers over a nipple and pinched it drawing a groan from his beloved.

He smiled and looked again at her breasts, and freckles thereupon. "I shall have to kiss every one of your delightful freckles."

Elizabeth giggled then gasped when he carried through on his promise. Mr. Darcy kissed and licked each freckle. It was difficult to hold his lower half of his body away, but he did not want her to feel his hard cock poking her side. He would not have Elizabeth scared of their marriage bed again.

Mr. Darcy moved down the bed while pulling down her silk nightdress, exposing freckles on her pale stomach that he also kissed. Elizabeth giggled and played with the curls on top of his head. As he grew closer to her legs, she pulled his hair.

"Fitzwilliam."

He ignored his wife and continued to kiss and move down.

"Fitzwilliam!"

The tugs on his hair were stronger and urgent. He looked up at her with a sly smile and opened his mouth—

"Fitzwilliam Darcy! I will not be treated in such an insolent manner by your Butler!"

CHAPTER 5

ELIZABETH STARTLED, yanking Mr. Darcy's head up by his hair. She let go with a gasp, horrified she had hurt him because he winced and was now holding a hand to his head.

"Nephew! I demand you speak to me."

She pulled at the covers to cover herself, but Mr. Darcy was still lying on top of them, preventing them from moving. Instead, she slid under the blankets and lay next to him. "What is she doing here? I thought she went to Lambton."

"Unhand me at once! My nephew has to house me! I have every right to be here."

Elizabeth hurriedly pulled up her nightdress and tried to put her arms in the holes while under the covers and unable to see. She felt her husband get off the bed, but then the blankets were suddenly raised, and he was staring at her.

"I am sorry Elizabeth, but I need to take care of my aunt." Mr. Darcy's visage was so ferocious that she almost felt pity for Lady Catherine. "I do not know what she is doing, but I plan to throw her out."

Elizabeth still did not want to be undressed in case his aunt barged in. It would be the height of rudeness and something she did not think Lady Catherine would do, but then again, she had not expected that woman would have dropped in on them on their wedding night.

Once she finally had her arms in her nightdress, she heard Mr. Darcy's bedchamber door slam. She was quite angry herself. Of all the times to be disturbed! Elizabeth blushed at what they had been doing, but she was vexed they had been interrupted. Now she would have to battle her nerves all over again. She covered her face with her hands and laughed. Were they ever going to consummate their marriage? Or would his aunt interrupt them again? Was she doing this on purpose?

Elizabeth stopped laughing and raised her head. Was that why she was here? To tell Fitzwilliam to get an annulment?

She frowned and threw the covers off. It was high time that woman knew that anything she did to separate them would be fruitless. Elizabeth got off the bed, put on her robe, slippers and left her bedchamber without slamming the door.

She did not hear distinct words, no more yelling, but she did perceive the sounds of a conversation most likely coming from the entrance or the main staircase. Elizabeth walked down the hall, glad there were no servants to see her in this thin robe. She held the top of her robe together, and with her long hair over her shoulders, she was thoroughly covered. If Lady Catherine became distressed at seeing her in her night clothes, then she should not have shown up this late after she had already been sent away.

"—travesty of an inn. I will not be treated thus by some no name establishment. It is far too late in the evening for someone of my stature to be wandering the county looking for a room when my nephew lives nearby in a grand house."

"You have insulted myself and my new wife. You appeared unexpectedly on the very evening we ourselves had just arrived, and now after insulting both me and my bride, you demand lodging? I suggest—"

"I have never been treated so badly as I have been by you, my own nephew today! You spurned my knowledge and advice to marry a lower-class, ill behaved hoyden. I arrived here—"

"You have a curious way of asking for a favor. You are not welcome and must leave immediately!"

Elizabeth was now at the top of the stairs but behind the corner of the hallway. Lady Catherine pulled herself up to her full height with a mean glare.

"Mr. Jameson, and any other servants listening, can you please escort her to her carriage?"

"How dare you treat me in this manner? I am the last living sister of your own dear mother and you defy me thusly? I—"

Mr. Darcy turned his back on his aunt and stepped up the staircase. By then the butler and footmen had reached Lady Catherine and were carrying her down the steps while avoiding her cane. That did not stop her complaints regarding Mr. Darcy ruining all his ancestors had worked for.

The man himself stopped suddenly when he came to the top of the staircase and saw Elizabeth.

"I am sorry, Fitzwilliam." She opened her arms to him, which Mr. Darcy rushed into with a weary smile.

They held each other before Elizabeth broached the subject, unsure of the response she would get. "Does she truly have nowhere else to go tonight?"

Mr. Darcy frowned. "She said there was no room suitable at the Lambton Inn. That could mean there were no accommodations or that the place was not acceptable to her."

She bit the inside of her cheek as she looked over Mr. Darcy's shoulder to the main staircase. Then she turned to him. "I love how you defended me, Fitzwilliam. You are an excellent husband. But do you think we should send her, an elderly woman, out on the dark country roads at this time of night? There are highwaymen, and even a setback with the carriage would be disastrous."

Elizabeth did not like the thought of showing charity to a woman that had just so abused them both, but she was also worried about the future of their family relations. Plus, what if highwaymen or an accident did befall Lady Catherine? She knew Mr. Darcy would never forgive himself.

He sighed and shifted to look back at the staircase. "She does not belong here for what she said about you." He turned back to Elizabeth. "But I do understand your concern."

Elizabeth smiled and held her husband in another embrace. Not only had Mr. Darcy listened to her, but he had changed his mind based on her reasoning. She kissed his cheek.

Mr. Darcy turned to her with a sparkle in his eyes. "I do not want her in the usual guest chambers on this floor. Where would you have her stay?"

"Are there other rooms that have not been used lately? In the other wing?"

Mr. Darcy's lips upturned. "I can have the servants get a room ready in the west wing, one of the guest suites that is utilized for house parties."

Elizabeth grinned. "I shall go back to my bedchamber and wait for you."

MR. DARCY FELT FOOLISH WALKING OUTSIDE AND calling for his servants to stop, but it was the right decision. No matter how angry he was at his aunt, Elizabeth was correct that throwing her out in the middle of the night was not to be done.

He waited in the entry for his aunt and held up his hand when she stormed back through the doors of Pemberley. "You are granted permission to stay here this night alone so that you will not come to harm on the roads. However, you are not allowed to leave your chamber until you leave for Rosings immediately in the morning. You will be served breakfast in your chamber."

Lady Catherine de Bourgh scowled, pursed her lips, then turned to one of the footmen and told him to bring her bags to her room.

"Mr. Jameson, if you could direct my aunt to the room the maids have prepared for her. Mr. Simkin, please inform Cook to send a breakfast tray to my aunt in the morning."

Lady Catherine was directed to the west wing of the house. The servants did their jobs, but by their unsmiling or even frowning countenances, they showed their displeasure with her behavior.

Mr. Darcy turned, climbed up the staircase, and walked back down the hall. He entered his room and stood in front of the connecting door to his wife's bedchamber. He ran his hand through his hair and sighed. He was tired and in pain due to having been so close to relief and denied two times that evening already. He could not attempt again to consummate the marriage that night. He hoped Elizabeth would not be upset. It was quite late, and hopefully she was fatigued as well.

Mr. Darcy went through the connecting door and found her tucked into bed. The covers were only up over her chest, and not up to her eyes this time. She smiled at him. "Did your aunt accept your offer?

Mr. Darcy walked around the room pinching out the candles. "She did. I can imagine how tired you are from traveling, and I think sleeping is the best course of action for tonight."

He pinched out the candle next to the bed and turned to see his wife staring at him with one eyebrow raised. "Husband, I was sure you understood that I like being involved in any decisions about my actions."

Mr. Darcy stood still but distinctively paler than he had been. "Elizabeth, I apologize. I did not think..." He ran his hands through his hair. "Are you tired?"

Elizabeth's countenance eased and her eyes twinkled. "Yes. Thank you. Could you stay here in my bed with me tonight? I enjoyed," Mr. Darcy noticed a blush upon her cheeks and neck, "our time together and do not want it to end, but only if we sleep. I am fatigued."

Mr. Darcy shed his robe and climbed in bed next to his wife. "I have longed for many months to hold you in my arms all night."

Elizabeth beamed and opened her arms. He moved over into his wife's embrace with a deep sigh of contentment and happiness.

CHAPTER 6

ELIZABETH WOKE warm and unable to move. It had not been difficult to get used to Mr. Darcy sleeping in the bed; she had shared with Jane until she was married. However, Jane had not been as hot as a furnace. But once Elizabeth had fallen asleep, it had been the best sleep she could remember. She stretched and snuggled back against her husband's chest.

"Good morning, Mrs. Darcy."

Elizabeth smiled and turned her head to see Mr. Darcy smiling at her from just a few inches away. "Good morning, Mr. Darcy."

He leaned forward and kissed her on the lips.

Elizabeth frowned. "Did your kiss have to be so quick?"

"I do not feel that I could stop if I kissed you with how I feel right now." His heavy-lidded gaze sent shivers up her body. "I will wait until my aunt is gone for sure." He rose his eyebrows. "Unless you would not mind celebrating our wedding night while Lady Catherine de Bourgh is in the house?"

Elizabeth blanched. "Definitely not. I bow to your superior judgment, husband." She giggled, then kissed him on the nose.

"I think I can say I have never been pecked on my nose before."

"Then it is a good thing that you have gotten yourself a wife."

Mr. Darcy smiled. "Shall we head down to break our fast together?"

Elizabeth's stomach rumbled, causing her to blush and Mr. Darcy to chuckle.

"I shall take that as a yes."

After another quick kiss they separated with Mr. Darcy walking to his bedchamber while Elizabeth rang the bell for her chambermaid. She blushed when she realized that the fire in the fireplace meant a maid had been in her room while they had been sleeping. A maid entering her bedchamber while she was sleeping had not been a problem at Longbourn, but now that she was married, she did not want anyone seeing them in bed. Especially when they were... doing what they did last night.

Elizabeth placed her hands on her burning cheeks. She would love to ask Jane how she had handled it, but their distance was too far. It would take getting used to being separated from her sister and best friend.

Her maid entered the bedchamber and quickly helped Elizabeth dress. When Elizabeth turned down the offer of a bath, she found herself explaining that she was too hungry to wait for one. At the maid's knowing look, Elizabeth blushed again. After her hair was done she rushed from the room to meet her husband in the hallway.

Mr. Darcy stood from a chair. "Shall we go down, my beautiful wife?"

Elizabeth smiled putting her arm through his. They both walked downstairs and into the dining room together. Everything on the buffet looked delicious, but Elizabeth chose a few of her favorites and sat down at Mr. Darcy's right side. At her husband's questioning look, she responded. "I have no desire to shout down the table to you. There are only two of us here for now, and we should sit near each other so we can converse."

Mr. Darcy nodded and swallowed his food. "When Georgianna is back from her visit with my aunt and uncle, the Matlocks, she can sit on my left side directly across from you."

Elizabeth smiled. She was the luckiest woman to have such a considerate husband. Again, she was amazed at the change in Mr. Darcy since the proposal at Hunsford. He was willing to listen to her ideas and heed her advice. She was sure they would have a long and happy marriage.

Their meal satisfactorily concluded, Mr. Darcy suggested a walk through the interior of Pemberley. "I know you had a short tour of the house when you visited with the Gardiners," he said as they both smiled at each other, "but I shall give you a tour of the entire house."

She did not mind a more thorough excursion through the grand house. It was beautiful and intimidating. Elizabeth was sure she would be lost many times in the next several weeks or months.

They passed servants cleaning and footmen running errands. She managed to stop her blushing after a few rooms, even though she was still embarrassed that she was sure all the servants knew what Mr. Darcy and she had been doing the night before. Not just the previous night, either, as he was a right devil teasing her during the tour.

He would wrap his arm around her waist and move his fingertips, trail fingers down her side and bottom when she turned, kiss her cheek or neck right in a room with servants, but when the staff were facing away. He was the most distracting part of the tour. It was amazing she could even remember any of the rooms she had seen.

In between the music room and the blue room, Mr. Jameson approached to tell them that Lady Catherine had eaten her morning meal in her bedchamber and was now leaving.

Elizabeth faced Mr. Darcy. "Should we send her off?"

Mr. Darcy shook his head. "No. Her visits were unexpected and boorish. Plus, she insulted you. We will continue with the tour of rooms."

Each room at Pemberley was a delightful look into Mr. Darcy's childhood and what had molded his personality. She had heard stories about the rooms and asked many questions, such as what was his favorite part and if he wanted to change any of it. She bit the inside of her cheek to keep from laughing when he would answer her as the staid landowner while running his fingers along her arm or back. He was a sneaky devil.

She managed to keep her mind on the tour, even though images of what they had done last night before being interrupted kept displaying in her head. She knew she would have to wait until that evening before a repeat and consoled herself that the end of the day would be there before she knew it.

THE FINAL ROOM WAS ONE HE KNEW WOULD BE Elizabeth's favorite. "And here is the Pemberley library."

He watched Elizabeth gasp and her eyes light up as she turned to take in the entire room. Every wall was covered with books. There were reading chairs in a grouping and a comfortable chaise lounge near the window, though the window was covered with thick curtains to keep the sun from damaging the books.

"Fitzwilliam, this is... outstanding."

He followed her around the room as she explored: picking up books, running her fingers along the spines and exclaiming when she found a first edition. Never had the library given him such enjoyment, and he had spent many happy hours there.

As Elizabeth studied a book, Mr. Darcy could not stop from trailing his fingers down her long neck. She looked up and smiled but bent over her book again. He smirked, as she would not be ignoring him for long. He had closed the library door when they had first entered, which was a signal to the servants that he was reading or researching and not to be interrupted.

Mr. Darcy trailed his hands down her back and around her side while he rested his other hand on her hip. He stepped closer and kissed the back of her neck by her brown curls and then continued down her neck until he reached the top of her dress.

"Mr. Darcy, you are distracting me."

He paused with his lips right above her skin. "Good. I am trying to distract you."

His fingers trailed along her side, her hips, then around to her stomach. But Elizabeth was determined to ignore him, although she giggled and hunched her right shoulder to prevent him from kissing the side of her neck. He chuckled and kissed down her neck, her collarbone, and her chest until he reached the edging of her dress. He trailed his other hand down the small of her back and rested it on her deliciously round rump.

"Fitzwilliam! The servants could see us."

Mr. Darcy chuckled and stood straight. "They will not. I do much reading and research in this library. They know that when the door is closed, they are not to disturb."

Elizabeth's eyes darted over to the door then back to him. "It is a public room of the house, is it not? And it is morning yet."

Mr. Darcy dragged a finger over her neck and up to her cheek that was hot with her blush. "The marriage bed can be celebrated any time of day or night and anywhere. Especially in the library."

Elizabeth scoffed.

"I know my wife well, and I know how much she loves books."

Mr. Darcy kissed her burning cheek, her neck, and downward to the edge of her dress. He knew this was

Elizabeth's favorite room in all of Pemberley. Which room would make her relaxed and not nervous, her bedchamber or the library?

Elizabeth gamely ignored him, but it was impossible when he squeezed her rump and nipped her breast over her dress. "Fitzwilliam! You have left a mark, and the fabric is wet. You have to stop this."

He stood up to drape an arm around her shoulders and directed her to the wide and comfortable chaise lounge. "I completely agree. We need to unbutton your dress and pull it down immediately."

Elizabeth gasped and stopped walking. "You could not."

Mr. Darcy smiled as he pulled off his coat and threw it aside.

"What are you doing?"

"I am doing exactly what I have wanted to do since I learned how much you loved to read while you were at Netherfield during your sister's illness."

The surprise of his declaration momentarily rendered her speechless, so Mr. Darcy was able to remove his vest and was working on removing his cravat when Elizabeth spoke again.

"You thought of me and have wanted me in your library since that long ago?"

Mr. Darcy nodded as he whipped off his cravat and threw it at the chair, though it missed, falling to the rug that covered the floor. "I have indeed. It became quite difficult to read in here, as I so badly wanted you in this room, reading in your own chair next to me."

He stepped close to his wife, rubbing his hands over her shoulders while he kissed her temple, her cheek-bone, and finally, her lips. "Could I interest you in lying down on the comfortable chaise lounge?"

He accompanied the request with a deep kiss, complete with rump squeezing and thumbing a nipple through her dress.

They both released each other from the passionate kiss, panting. Elizabeth glanced again at the door and then back at him. "The chaise does look quite comfortable."

Mr. Darcy grinned.

"Could you unbutton me?" she asked.

"I would be glad to act as your maid." He walked behind her and quickly unbuttoned her dress and chemise. He pulled her dress up and off with a gasp from Elizabeth.

"I thought we were going to have our clothes on! You have your clothes on!"

He stifled his chuckle as he realized Elizabeth was standing with her arms crossed over her chest, staring at the door.

"We are not going to remove all of our clothes. Besides, I would not be able to see your breasts with that confining dress on."

Elizabeth gave him a flat stare. "I believe you are much too fascinated by my breasts, sirrah."

He raised his eyebrows as he put his hands on her shoulders and kissed her forehead, her cheek, her lips. "I do not think I am fascinated enough."

Mr. Darcy walked her to the chaise and laid down next to her, his back facing the door and blocking any view of it for Elizabeth. She relaxed and then smiled, holding her arms open for him.

They were so enamored of their mutual exploration that they did not hear the front door of Pemberley burst open with the familiar voice of Lady Catherine de Bourgh.

CHAPTER 7

MR. JAMESON HAD BEEN SURPRISED by Lady Catherine de Bourgh's abrupt appearance at Pemberley, again. But he quickly recovered and rushed to stand in front of her. "Your Ladyship, Mr. Darcy is not available."

She had been glaring at the butler but now raised herself to her full height with an added chin raise. "Bring me to my nephew at once."

Mr. Jameson, already standing tall, pushed his shoulders back and added a chin tilt of his own. "I am afraid Mr. Darcy is not to be disturbed. You have been asked by him to leave the premises this morning, therefore I must ask you to leave again."

Mrs. Reynolds the housekeeper rushed across the entryway to stand next to the butler. They were now a wall, preventing Lady Catherine from accessing Pemberley.

Lady Catherine glared at them both. "Bring me to Mr. Darcy at once!"

Mrs. Reynolds pursed her lips. "As Mr. Jameson said, Mr. Darcy is not available. You must leave the premises."

"Are you going to deny me seeing my nephew when his aunt is in need of assistance?"

Mr. Jameson looked heavenwards as Mrs. Reynolds answered. "Your Ladyship, you are aware of Mr. Darcy's wishes regarding your unexpected arrivals at Pemberley. He does not wish you to stay here and does not prefer you to enter the house."

Lady Catherine de Bourgh banged her cane upon the marble floor. Mrs. Reynolds frowned and clenched her fists as she looked down at the marble treated so abominably by her ladyship.

"You would like me to go then?"

Mr. Jameson narrowed his eyes and nodded.

Lady Catherine swung her arm out towards the front door. "Well, go out and look! Tell me how I am to leave Pemberley?"

Both the butler and housekeeper shared a look. The butler walked past Lady Catherine, opened the front door and walked out. There was no carriage with the de Bourgh coat of arms.

There was, however, a phaeton with a young dandy in the driver's seat. At seeing the butler, he yelled out. "Her Ladyship said she knows the owner of Pemberley and that I could expect a reward for delivering her here."

The butler closed his eyes and groaned. He opened them again to see one of the dandy's high-spirited horses side stepping and pulling at the bit, taking all the dandy's attention.

He closed the door and turned with a motion for Mrs. Reynolds to come to him. Mrs. Reynolds in turn motioned for a footman to stand near Lady Catherine before she walked over to Mr. Jameson.

"Her carriage is not here. There is a dandy in a phaeton that is awaiting a reward that Lady Catherine promised him for delivering her Ladyship to Pemberley."

Mrs. Reynolds closed her eyes and sighed. "I will see to the reward for the man. We will have to find out what the problem is with Lady Catherine's carriage. Perhaps we can still help her leave the county."

ELIZABETH WAS STILL AMAZED THAT SHE WAS almost entirely unclothed in the library during the day with her husband. She bit her cheek to stop a giggle at the thought of writing Jane about Mr. Darcy convincing her that the marriage bed could be had during daytime, in the library, and could still be proper.

Her musings were forced out of her head by Mr. Darcy reaching into her chemise and reverently lifting out both breasts. Elizabeth bit the inside of her cheek to keep from laughing at how he stared at them like they were the crown jewels. Her amusement turned to exquisite pleasure when Mr. Darcy kissed and licked her nipples. He squeezed and fondled them while groaning.

Elizabeth ran her hands through the curls of his hair and wished she could reach his chest or some part of him other than just the top of his head. She did enjoy his attention to her body, but she wanted to examine him as well.

"Fitzwilliam," she said, lightly tugging his hair, "I

would like to explore you as well. Could you come up here?"

She did not think he had heard her, but Mr. Darcy groaned and slowly moved up, lying on his side next to her on the chaise facing Elizabeth. She giggled at his pout. "There is more to me than just my chest, Mr. Darcy."

He leaned over and kissed her with deep and passionate fervor. "I know. I plan to explore every inch of you."

Elizabeth was breathing heavily from the kiss, but that did not stop her from unbuttoning his shirt. She pulled the sides apart gazed at his muscular chest and hair. "You are so muscled!"

"You did not expect that?"

Elizabeth shook her head while she lightly trailed her fingers over his chest. "I did not. You are a land owner." That was all she could manage to get out with how distracted she was by his chest and stomach. She was fascinated with the movement of his muscles as she dragged her fingers over them. If Miss Bingley knew of the fine physique that she had missed out on with Mr. Darcy, the woman would wail and gnash her teeth forever.

"I am not idle like many of the upper class. I fence, I ride, I—" Mr. Darcy grabbed Elizabeth's hand before she brushed against the hard perturbance in his breeches.

"I fear if you touch me there, I will not be able to stop myself. I want to get you ready before I allow you to do that."

Elizabeth nodded though she was quite confused as to what he meant. He would not be able to stop, and she had to get ready? What a bizarre thing this marriage bed must be.

Mr. Darcy pulled her chemise up. Elizabeth squeezed his shoulder and the chaise to keep herself from covering her woman parts with her hands.

"Do not be frightened. There is nothing to be frightened of."

"No man has ever seen this part of me."

Mr. Darcy smiled and gazed at her from under heavy-lidded eyes while he pulled her chemise up to the top of her thighs. He trailed his fingers down her thighs, leaving hot tingles and making her fidget. When he ran his fingers through her curls, she jumped.

Mr. Darcy chuckled.

"It is not funny."

He kissed her stomach which caused Elizabeth to gasp. He dragged his fingers over her stomach, through her curls, over her legs. Then he slowly pushed her legs apart with his hand and continued exploring. She jumped again when his fingers reached deeper into her curls.

She cried out and dug her fingers deeper into his shoulder. "What are you doing?"

"I am making you feel good." He leaned over and kissed her slowly, deeply while he pushed a finger inside her.

Elizabeth was startled, but she could not jump with his weight on her chest. Mr. Darcy moved his finger in and out, circling, driving her mad. Her body was screaming for him, for something to go in there. She felt like a wanton lightskirt, spreading her legs wider. She knew not why she spread her legs, it just felt like the right thing to do.

"Oh, Fitzwilliam!" Elizabeth was panting. She was overcome by so many strong urges. She hoped Mr. Darcy did not think her wanton. Truly, she had not done anything like this. And she had not even seen all of him yet.

THE BUTLER AND HOUSEKEEPER LEARNED THAT Lady Catherine de Bourgh's carriage had a broken axle a good ways away, at least ten miles. It was not near any town that could repair the carriage. Her luggage and servants would have to be moved to another carriage and her broken carriage rigged to be able to be pulled behind.

Mr. Jameson approached Lady Catherine and informed her of the plans to retrieve her belongings and have the carriage repaired.

"Well, it seems as if my nephew has employed decent servants after all."

Mrs. Reynolds frowned and pursed her lips.

"If you could bring refreshments to the music room, I will be waiting there to speak with my nephew." Lady Catherine de Bourgh walked around Mrs. Reynolds and up a step of the staircase.

"Lady Catherine, you need to go with the carriage to direct them to where your carriage is broken down. It will not be repaired here at Pemberley, but at Lambton, and you will need to be with it."

Lady Catherine did not even stop her ascent of the staircase. "Nonsense."

Mrs. Reynolds rushed to the entry wall and pulled the bell so that footmen would arrive to help her with Mr. Darcy's recalcitrant aunt.

MR. DARCY TRIED TO CALM HIMSELF BY SLOWLY breathing through his mouth, but it was not working. He had wanted Elizabeth for so long, and she was calling out his name. He was shaking from his need, his desire. His finger came away from her slick.

He unbuttoned his breeches but did not pull them down, not yet. "I must warn you, I... this part of a man's body is... it may seem rather big, and... do not fear."

He could have smacked himself for being so incoherent. He had probably scared her instead of reassuring her. Mr. Darcy pulled his breeches down with a sigh of relief as he was fully exposed and no longer confined. At the cry from Elizabeth he opened his eyes. "What is wrong?"

She was staring at that part of his body that yearned for her touch.

He chuckled.

Elizabeth looked up at him with a frown. "Is that supposed to go in me? That is not going to work. There is not a possible way that is going in me!"

He smiled, but it dimmed when he realized she was truly frightened. Mr. Darcy trailed his fingers along her hair, down her side, and over the smooth skin of her hip. "Put your hand on the point and feel. It is soft."

Elizabeth still stared with fear but gamely reached out a finger and touched the point, drawing a deep groan from him.

"Oh no, did I hurt you?"

He shook his head with his eyes still closed. He was afraid that if he opened them and saw her delicate fingers near his cock, he would explode. "You did not hurt me, but you made me feel quite good. Please touch me again."

Mr. Darcy breathed heavily through his nose while conjugating Latin verbs, thinking of the fall harvest yields, anything at all except for Elizabeth's soft fingers on his cock. Finally, he groaned and opened his eyes. He was shaking from need. He could not take it anymore.

"My love I have to be inside you now."

Thankfully she did not look as frightened as she had several minutes ago. He pushed her legs wider and positioned himself over her and his cock at her entrance. Then with a deep groan, he slowly pushed in. He stopped when immediately Elizabeth gasped. He was in exquisite pleasure, but he would not move if she was in pain. "Tell me when you feel better, when it does not hurt as much."

"Oh, it does not hurt now. It is such an odd feeling."

He grinned but with shaking arms, he could not hold himself still anymore. He eased in deeper as Elizabeth gasped and squirmed, which made it even more difficult for him to be careful with his new bride. He felt her hands on his back as her breasts tickled the hair on his chest. He bit the inside of his cheek so hard he tasted blood. "Are you comfortable? Can I move?"

"Yes. You are in pain! I am sorry. I did not know this would hurt you."

He shook his head. His eyes were closed, as he knew if he saw her under him, he would lose all control. "It is painful keeping myself still."

"Then please move. I do not want you in pain."

He moved. Slowly in, easing almost out and then back in again, increasing the tempo. He lost himself in her when she moaned and dug her fingers into his back with her cries. He feathered her forehead and hair with kisses, then gave over entirely to the pleasure, the joy of feeling Elizabeth at Pemberley at last.

LADY CATHERINE DE BOURGH WAS SPRY FOR HER age. She climbed the staircase and walked down the hall to the library without any footman approaching her. She knew her nephew would be in his favorite room.

Fitzwilliam would not expect her to ride in the carriage back to her broken carriage. He would especially not make her go to Lambton for repairs. She could not imagine anyone in Lambton, such a small village, to be qualified to repair a well sprung carriage such as hers.

She smiled at the sound of rapid steps up the staircase. Lady Catherine walked faster, amused at surprising the servants that she was not a doddering old woman.

Mr. Darcy groaned as stars exploded behind his eyes. He called out Elizabeth's name and collapsed. He was spent, drained of any and all energy. He shuffled off her so he was lying mainly on his side, his back facing the door with his breeches down around his knees. His right arm was thrown over her stomach as he panted in her ear.

Elizabeth pulled her chemise down over her hips and slowly moved her legs closer together while she herself breathed heavily.

Neither of them could hear anything over their loud breathing. Nor did either of them have a view of the door to the library. Which was why they did not see the well oiled library door open to admit Lady Catherine de Bourgh.

CHAPTER 8

LADY CATHERINE DE BOURGH, the scion of the well established and grand estate of Rosings Park, blanched at the view that greeted her. Her cane slipped out of her hand to land on the thick rug, muting the sound of its landing. She clutched her favorite pearls and fainted dead away.

"Fitzwilliam, did you hear something?"

Mr. Darcy, still breathing heavy, shook his head. "I hear nothing except my own breathing."

THE FOOTMEN HAD RUN DOWN THE HALL BUT WERE just too late to catch Mr. Darcy's aunt as she fell. One servant opened his mouth, but a sharp poke in his ribs had him turn to the other, who held up a finger over his lips and was gesticulating wildly. The first footman still did not understand, so the other servant's hand covered his mouth and turned his head towards the library interior.

After that, both quickly dragged her ladyship out of the library into the hall and slowly and silently closed the library door. By now, Mrs. Reynolds had appeared, but with a finger over his lips and big eyes from the first footman, she understood immediately what had caused Lady Catherine to faint.

Completely silent and only using hand gestures, Mrs. Reynolds directed them to bring her ladyship to the bedchamber she had used the night before. Footmen departed with the dandy in the phaeton, along with a carriage, to bring back the broken de Bourgh carriage, luggage and servants.

There was no obvious trauma to her ladyship's head, but to be safe, they sent for the physician to examine her. If she did not wake by the next day, he was to be called again. Until then, they were doing everything correctly.

Mr. Jameson and Mrs. Reynolds breathed sighs of relief.

Mr. Darcy and Elizabeth, after a comfortable nap, stood up from the chaise lounge. They helped each other button and straighten their clothing.

"I am glad that you removed my dress. I can not imagine how wrinkled it would be if you had not."

Mr. Darcy quit trying to tie his cravat and smiled at his wife. "Do you happen to know anything about cravats?"

Elizabeth turned for him to button her up, which he did. Then she surprised him by turning around and quickly tying his cravat in a simple knot. "I would have to help my father with his cravat every Sunday before church. It is not as elaborate as your valet can achieve, but it is at least respectable."

Mr. Darcy reached for Elizabeth's arm, put it through his, and walked to the library door.

Elizabeth bit the inside of her cheek so she would not blush and it would look as if nothing at all was amiss and that they had just read books or such in the library.

The couple walked down the stairs, as they were both famished. At the bottom of the stairs stood both Mr.

Jameson and Mrs. Reynolds. That was unusual unless something had happened, but the odd looks on their countenances worried Mr. Darcy.

"Mr. Darcy," stated the butler, "your aunt arrived again due to a broken axle on her carriage. I took the liberty of sending another carriage to collect her belongings and tow her carriage back."

Mr. Darcy blinked. It was too quiet for his aunt to be at Pemberley. "Where is my aunt now?"

Again, the housekeeper and butler shared looks before the housekeeper answered. "It is unfortunate, but she fainted and fell. I placed her in the same room she used last night and called the physician. She has no obvious trauma or head injury and is resting comfortably."

"Is that due to the carriage accident?"

Mrs. Reynolds paused before answering, which was unusual. "It seems she mis-stepped off the edge of a rug and fell. She wanted me to deliver a message to you. She says she is quite fine and will rest in her bedchamber so she does not disturb you. She wanted to make sure you knew not to visit her or change your schedule for her."

Mr. Darcy raised his eyebrows and blinked. He turned to Elizabeth who was also speechless. Then he turned back to his butler and housekeeper with a smirk. "It seems as if my aunt might have learned something after all."

Mr. Jameson coughed.

Mrs. Reynolds looked down at the floor then back up at Mr. Darcy with a blank countenance. "I believe she did, Mr. Darcy."

Mr. Darcy narrowed his eyes at the both of them. They were keeping something from him, but he trusted them both completely, as they had been working at Pemberley since before he was born. When his stomach rumbled, he decided to let the matter go. If he needed to be informed, one of them would do it. He was sure, however, that his aunt had yelled insults at his staff and nothing else had occurred.

Mr. Darcy nodded at them both, then led Elizabeth towards the dining room for another one of Cook's delicious meals.

The End.

Made in the USA
Coppell, TX
25 October 2023

23346387R00052